On the Way to the Pond

On the

Way to the Pond

Angela Shelf Medearis

Illustrated by Lorinda Bryan Cauley

Green Light Readers
Harcourt, Inc.

Orlando Austin New York San Diego Toronto London

One day, Tess Tiger went to visit Herbert Hippo. They were hungry. Herbert packed a big basket for a picnic at the pond. It was full of good food.

"You bring the lunch," said Tess. "I'll bring these four very important things."
Herbert looked at them and just nodded.

They started up the path. It was a very hot day. All of a sudden, Herbert felt sick.

"Sit under my umbrella," said Tess.
"I'll fan you."
"Thanks," said Herbert.

When Herbert felt better, they went off to the pond. All of a sudden, Herbert stopped and cried, "Oh no! I forgot the basket!"

"I'll go back and get it," said Tess. "You go on."

Tess dropped some rocks as she walked. She found the picnic basket and turned to go back.

On the way, Tess stopped. First she looked this way. Then she looked that way. She was lost!

"It's a good thing I dropped these rocks," she said. "I'll just follow them back."

Tess got to the pond, but she couldn't find Herbert. "Oh no! Herbert is lost!" She got out her whistle. *R-r-r-r-r-r!*

"Here I am!" cried Herbert.
"I'm glad you had all that important stuff!"

"Yes," said Tess, "and I'm glad you packed a big lunch! I'm starving!"

I Can Do This!

Tess Tiger and Herbert Hippo are good friends. They like to do things together. Make a book to show what special things you can do with your family and friends.

WHAT YOU'LL NEED

paper

crayons or markers

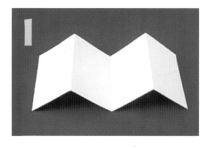

Fold a big sheet of paper to make an accordion book.

Make a cover.

Draw pictures of things you can do with your family and friends.

Share your book with a group.

Make a Picnic Snack

Herbert packed lots of good food for his picnic with Tess. If you go on a picnic, bring along this tasty snack!

WHAT YOU'LL NEED

pretzels   **raisins**   **popcorn**   **nuts**

small plastic bags   **measuring cup**   **large self-closing plastic bags**

3 cups popcorn

1 cup nuts

2 cups pretzels

2 cups raisins

- Measure each ingredient and pour them into a large plastic bag.

- Close the bag. Shake the bag to mix up your snack.

- Pour or scoop out the snack into small bags.

Now you and your friends have a delicious

picnic snack!

Meet the Author and Illustrator

Angela Shelf Medearis loves to laugh and write silly stories. She has an office filled with toys. The toys give her ideas and make her laugh. She hopes that *On the Way to the Pond* puts a smile on your face.

Angela Shelf Medearis

It takes Lorinda Bryan Cauley about four days to draw the picture for one page of a book. First she does pencil drawings. Then she adds color with colored pencils and colored ink. Lorinda works very hard on the characters' eyes. She thinks the eyes are very important for showing feelings. What do you think?

Lorinda Bryan Cauley

Requests for permission to make copies of any part of the work should be mailed to the following address: Permissions Department, Harcourt, Inc., 6277 Sea Harbor Drive, Orlando, Florida 32887-6777.

www.HarcourtBooks.com

First Green Light Readers edition 2006

Green Light Readers is a trademark of Harcourt, Inc., registered in the United States of America and/or other jurisdictions.

Library of Congress Cataloging-in-Publication Data
Medearis, Angela Shelf, 1956–
On the way to the pond/written by Angela Shelf Medearis; illustrated by Lorinda Bryan Cauley.
p. cm.
"Green Light Readers."
Summary: While going on a picnic together, Herbert Hippo teases Tess Tiger about all of the things she has brought along, until he learns just how important they can be.
[1. Preparedness—Fiction. 2. Picnicking—Fiction. 3. Tigers—Fiction.
4. Hippopotamus—Fiction.] I. Cauley, Lorinda Bryan, ill. II. Title. III. Series: Green Light reader.
PZ7.M51274On 2006
[E]—dc22   2005006937
ISBN-13: 978-0152-05599-8 ISBN-10: 0-15-205599-1
ISBN-13: 978-0152-05623-0 (pb) ISBN-10: 0-15-205623-8 (pb)

A C E G H F D B
A C E G H F D B (pb)

Ages 5–7
Grade: 1
Guided Reading Level: E
Reading Recovery Level: 7–8

Green Light Readers
For the reader who's ready to GO!

"A must-have for any family with a beginning reader."—*Boston Sunday Herald*

"You can't go wrong with adding several copies of these terrific books to your beginning-to-read collection."—*School Library Journal*

"A winner for the beginner."—*Booklist*

Five Tips to Help Your Child Become a Great Reader

1. Get involved. Reading aloud to and with your child is just as important as encouraging your child to read independently.

2. Be curious. Ask questions about what your child is reading.

3. Make reading fun. Allow your child to pick books on subjects that interest her or him.

4. Words are everywhere—not just in books. Practice reading signs, packages, and cereal boxes with your child.

5. Set a good example. Make sure your child sees YOU reading.

Why Green Light Readers Is the Best Series for Your New Reader

● Created exclusively for beginning readers by some of the biggest and brightest names in children's books

● Reinforces the reading skills your child is learning in school

● Encourages children to read—and finish—books by themselves

● Offers extra enrichment through fun, age-appropriate activities unique to each story

● Incorporates characteristics of the Reading Recovery program used by educators

● Developed with Harcourt School Publishers and credentialed educational consultants

Daniel's Mystery Egg
Alma Flor Ada/G. Brian Karas

Moving Day
Anthony G. Brandon/Wong Herbert Yee

My Robot
Eve Bunting/Dagmar Fehlau

Animals on the Go
Jessica Brett/Richard Cowdrey

Marco's Run
Wesley Cartier/Reynold Ruffins

Digger Pig and the Turnip
Caron Lee Cohen/Christopher Denise

Tumbleweed Stew
Susan Stevens Crummel/Janet Stevens

The Chick That Wouldn't Hatch
Claire Daniel/Lisa Campbell Ernst

Splash!
Ariane Dewey/Jose Aruego

Get That Pest!
Erin Douglas/Wong Herbert Yee

My Wild Woolly
Deborah J. Eaton/G. Brian Karas

A Place for Nicholas
Lucy Floyd/David McPhail

Why the Frog Has Big Eyes
Betsy Franco/Joung Un Kim

I Wonder
Tana Hoban

A Bed Full of Cats
Holly Keller

The Fox and the Stork
Gerald McDermott

Try Your Best
Robert McKissack/Joe Cepeda

Lucy's Quiet Book
Angela Shelf Medearis/Lisa Campbell Ernst

On the Way to the Pond
Angela Shelf Medearis/Lorinda Bryan Cauley

Tomás Rivera
Jane Medina/Edward Martinez

Boots for Beth
Alex Moran/Lisa Campbell Ernst

Catch Me If You Can!
Bernard Most

The Very Boastful Kangaroo
Bernard Most

Skimper-Scamper
Jeff Newell/Barbara Hranilovich

Farmers Market
Carmen Parks/Edward Martinez

Shoe Town
Janet Stevens/Susan Stevens Crummel

The Enormous Turnip
Alexei Tolstoy/Scott Goto

Where Do Frogs Come From?
Alex Vern

The Purple Snerd
Rozanne Lanczak Williams/Mary GrandPré

Did You See Chip?
Wong Herbert Yee/Laura Ovresat

Look for more Green Light Readers wherever books are sold!